Becka's Buckra Baby

Becka's
Buckra Baby

Thomas MacDermot

MINT EDITIONS

Becka's Buckra Baby was first published in 1903.

This edition published by Mint Editions 2021.

ISBN 9781513282725 | E-ISBN 9781513287744

Published by Mint Editions®

 MINT
EDITIONS

minteditionbooks.com

Publishing Director: Jennifer Newens
Design & Production: Rachel Lopez Metzger
Project Manager: Micaela Clark
Typesetting: Westchester Publishing Services

Contents

Madonna

The Night on the Town has fallen,
    And the Gar Lamps, few and far,
Out-flame like the picket fires
    On the rim of a lonely war.

The lights of the Town, Madonna,
    Are the eyes of a Soul's despair;
The streets are the thoughts, Madonna,
    That are dreary and dark and bare.

The lights that the World affords us,
    Though we win where they burn their best
Reveal but the pain, the hurry,
    The stir of a street's unrest.

And we turn from the street's confusion,
    From the toil and the City's pain,
From all that the heart desires.
    And all that the hand can gain:

For what if we win it or lose it,
    The praise that the World bestows,
It fades like a flower gathered,
    It dies like a withering rose.

Ah, the calm of God, Madonna,
    It is far from the streets away,
And seeking that calm. Madonna,
    The hearts of thy children stray.

                Thomas MacDermot
                Jamaica.

I

The Father of Noel

All the rough world passed by,
All that it could not try,
When it weighed act with act,
And balanced fact with fact.

Noel Maud Bronvola, this was her name, and she could hardly ever remember repeating it to another in full without hearing the following comment expressed, or seeing it suppressed in the eyes that regarded her:—

"Noel, for a girl?" And then her mother was want to reply:

"Yes, her father would have it. so. She was born on Christmas Day."

Every one, who knew him, or nearly every one, had said that Jack Bronvola was a peculiar man; and they were not slow to tell his peculiarities in detail, if you cared to hear them.

He gained a position in business while still a young man which meant for him in a decade or two, a fortune equal to any in the Island. That position he resigned a month or two after Noel's birth, because he considered the policy that he was called upon to execute, was unjust and cruel. Men generally find good reasons for not resigning £1,000 a year, steadily increasing to thrice that amount; and a man who does otherwise must justly be considered peculiar.

He was a man whose ability no one ever cared to dispute; and his family connections were influential and far reaching. Other positions scarcely less good were something more than open to him; but they had their objections, as he saw matters, and the end was, that he secured a post under Government which was worth barely £300, to start with.

Still the way lay clear before him for ascent. His ability soon told, and his prospects of early promotion grew bright. But unkind Fortune again interfered, and brought another opportunity for the exercise of that peculiar mind of Bronvola's.

Among his subs was a youngster whose father was a Magnate of the largest dimensions, literally and in a proprietorial sense, and of a power and influence not below those of any man between sea and sea through all Jamaica. All of which did not prevent the Magnate's youngster being a scoundrel of the first water. He drank, to the confusion of office work, and Bronvola rated him; he gambled, and this peculiar man both warned him and watched him. When it came to embezzlement, Bronvola put his hand out and crushed the young fool—like a fly.

So directly and carefully did he move, and with a determination so composed and unshakably firm, that, willing as the Authorities, or some of them, might have been, in view of the Magnate's, greatness, to let the quarry break the net and escape, they dared not allow it; and so prison doors received the Magnate's son on the day when they received the son of old Christie Downley, Parade and Sollas Market higgler, convicted of burglary in a Kingston suburb and of carrying off a watch and £5.

"Both thieves," said Bronvola and was satisfied.

Yet common-sense told him, and, as he knew it would, Time ultimately proved it true to him, that he on this day struck dead his chance of promotion. The Magnate's arm might be too short to save. It was quite long enough to destroy; and his hate was as long as his life. Bronvola, a man of serene soul, met his hate without a tremor; and lived without bitterness towards the Governors who feared the Magnate more than they feared God.

Noel was only twelve when her father died. For many years she knew of Jamaica only what Kingston, reveals; yet she loved the Island, and this intense love was wonderful; for Kingston is in ugliness past all endurance, and in wickedness beyond all imagination. Her father had been posted in the City and there he died in the full tide of his days, his life laid down unshrinkingly to redeem that of his daughter.

Noel lay sick of Diphtheria and was dying when her father saved her life and lost his own by sucking the breathing tube clear of the deadly fungus. He did it calmly, quietly, without outward sign that the heroic resolve he had taken was more than ordinary.

"It probably means death," the Doctor said, warning thus a man who he knew required no warning.

"I know," replied Bronvola, and did the deed of salvation for her and of death for himself.

Noel, still weak and wan from the struggle with the Mortal Foe, had at the very last when the end came for her Father, clung to him with a kiss that seemed to drive the two lives into one, like two flames commingling. She was too truly his daughter, and his mother had been too truly his helpmate and too thoroughly understood him, to thank him, or to praise that last great sacrifice. The wife joined hands with the Doctor and did all that skill and knowledge could to give the victory and life to the man who had dared to meet and face Death at the moment when His prey seemed irrevocably his own; but never once had she spoken what she thought and felt concerning that deed of self-sacrifice and supreme daring. Between father and mother and daughter there was the communion of souls. Words were not needed.

When Noel gave him that last, long, lingering, passionate kiss, her words were the simplest she could utter. She said,

"Good-bye, Father." But the eyes that poured their gaze on his spoke as the pure Angels of God speak, naked life to naked life; and the eyes of the dying man spoke back to her in full understanding, and with the deep, untroubled peace and flawless trust of the Soul that has been true to the Light.

So out into the Unknown passed the life of John Bronvola; and in the great heart of a girl there remained abiding the priceless resolution to follow worthily after that Soul into which her own had twice flown, at the mystic borders of Life and Death; to follow worthily and well, through things temporal and transitory, to pass with his untroubled peace, into things unseen and eternal. A priceless deed, that deed of Bronvola; never publicly acclaimed by pen or pulpit, known to men and women fewer than one counts fingers on a hand; but to reach to and through the great distance of years, and to be felt in lives innumerable.

The last struggle had quivered into quietude and perfect rest; the last, faint gasp of life on the hitherward side of the Vail was hushed and ended; the Widow wept softly as she prayed; and, from the lingering by the dead, an anxious Nurse strove to lead Noel away, dreading lest, weak as she was, Death should turn ere he left that house of Life and strike her also—it was then that perhaps by some sudden touch of God's hand upon his brain the old Clergyman who stood with these women in the Chamber of Death spoke the words "Greater love hath no man than this, that a man lay down his life for his friend." This he said, not knowing what manner of death Bronvola had died: but pointing these latest born of the Children of Sorrow to "a hill named Calvary." But surely it did not put them further from the Saviour of the World that mother and daughter were brought by the sublimely simple and pathetic words into the presence of a nearer sacrifice.

So passed Jack Bronvola, a man whom the world termed eccentric and peculiar, and very correctly so; for eccentricity is relative, and depends on where we place the centre; and peculiarity is relative and depends on what we make the standard.

The money that he left his wife and only child, gave them decent support, since he owned the house in which he passed from this life; but it allowed little to be laid out in the luxury of travelling, and thus it was destiny for Noel to pass her girlhood in Kingston. They had not many friends, the Bronvolas. A man who begins with £300 and ends with £1,000 will have no lack of friends. And he who has his £300 and sticks to it all through, will not be without some friends; but the man who has £1,000 and descends to £300; then with his own hand bars a re-ascent, that man will have few friends, indeed; a sordid bit of fact this.

II

Noel Herself

"Mixed————
In spite of the mortal screen."

J ack, his wife and Noel were very happy, almost perfectly so, till it pleased God to take the father; then the mother and the daughter went forward again, less happy in that he was no longer with them in the flesh; but all in all to each other, and sufficient.

And so year after year passed away, and there came for the two in due portion the sorrows, the pain, the anxieties, and the labour that fill up human life. But, till her girl was seventeen, the Mother could say with truth and gratitude that Noel had never grieved her heart. She had her father's strong, steady temper. Like him, she would get to reasons and neglect appearances, if they had no worthy justification. Like him, the currents of her mind swept from the first in that deep and resistless flow that broke neither into bitterness nor anger. And, to train such a heart, her mother was exactly the mother needed. Like the deep of the star sown sky, with its wide spaces and with the snow-white cloud drift, above plains where in the calm hush the buds are swelling into blossom—about the daughter's life the influence of the mother dwelt; and her girl's growth was like that of the lilies that toil not neither do they spin.

She had ways, had Noel, that a stranger prying into the home, would have pronounced odd; but to the two whose hearts dwelt there they were but sweet and natural.

Her father's Study remained as he had left it, with his books and pictures where he had set them; and there the many treasures he had been fond of assembling round him, cunning bits of wood-work, curiously grained stones, specimens of rare seeds, all were still kept in the places they had occupied when, in the midst of them all, sat Jack Bronvola, before and after office hours, writing, thinking or talking to his wife, or to his little eleven year old daughter.

Noel took charge of the Study after his death; she kept the key; her fingers alone dusted and replaced the table ornaments; and the books were removed from the big shelves by her arms only. Here she often came and sat for hours; sometimes with her mother beside her, and sometimes alone so far as a bodily presence went. On the table, day after, day she placed fresh flowers, and there they glowed, a flame from the invisible Spirit of Life that moves in the earth's dust and ashes, and changes death into life, the seed into the plant and from the murk of the clay calls the beauty of the flower. On the dead man's table the flowers, varying with the varying season, but daily renewed by unfailing love, burnt like the fires that in some Temples of God are never allowed to quench themselves in darkness, but speak the thought of Him that never fails, though the generations fail and pass; and to that thought types the Mystery that is from everlasting to everlasting.

Often when mother and daughter sat in the early darkness of night— on the vine-covered verandah, the house lamps burning low behind them, and the big stars above, answering with their steady light, to the gas glitter that the town showed here and there to illumine her darkness—while to the noises that street and lane flung up were returned the reaches of abiding silence—often then Noel would place a second chair, her father's, beside her mother's, and leaving it empty, go back to her own, to talk, or sing, or listen; just as of old they had done, when they were three, and when the second rocking chair was not empty where it stood. At such hours He was again with them.

The great thoughts of Great Poets, of the students of Life, the Novelist, the Philosopher, the Prophet, these came and went in their talk, casting no shame, imposing no insignificance on the ordinary affairs of their immediate lives, of the house, the town, the school, of friends and acquaintances; the beggars that came to the gate, the noise that rose from the streets—mention of which mingled also with their evening talks. All themes seemed to meet and interblend without jar or collision; as why should they not; and as they will whenever we win to Nature's way, and lay aside man's affectation and convention—since every bit is part of the Whole, and the beggar feeding his life with his crust is an integral bit of a discussion of the Immortality of the Soul and of the Infinite. Life is the garment woven from hem to hem, without seam.

But Nature has her work to do with us and she does it, while flesh and blood endure, and in seed time and in harvest; and when, at sixteen, Noel closed such books as we learn from in the Schools, there was arising, that within her that came to lead her to the larger pages of the great Book of Life. That other learning was to begin for her, and to lead

THOMAS MACDERMOT

her further than it is the general lot of women to go; and as it brings truth that is far more valuable when gained, so is it learning far more dangerous in the gaining.

She stood erect at sixteen in a beauty that showed nor spot nor wrinkle. Truth and purity, and the fearlessness these two create, dwelt in the clearness of her brown eyes. The true proportion of all the face, from the fine, full forehead to the dainty but firm chin, flung the beholder into no need of resting admiration on any one feature. Complete and entire as it was, the beauty before him conquered his admiration at once; and in beholding Noel one never said:

"What beautiful eyes; what perfect lips"—but,

"What a beautiful girl." "What a Life."

She had what is rare with the West Indian, white, black or brown, features in all but perfect proportion; for the West Indian girl, often good-looking, is seldom beautiful, if in beauty we demand as an essential fine proportion of form and feature. She had, what must be said to be rare in all women, a spirit akin to Nature's calm, and of that strength so unconscious, so full, set towards great issues, and working them out amid the ordinary and commonplace, without fret or jar, or sense of indignity.

Such a girl goes forth to be tried and tested by Life, and by the World's rough hands,—to win only a fool's reward—riches, position, praise from the lips of men, power; or, with these or without them, to receive honour, the praise that does not tabernacle in words, and the life eternal. Her fall, if she fall, shall be deep as Hell. If she endure, she indeed shall stand redeemed while yet in the flesh; and but a little lower than the angels that see God.

Noel's first contact with outside life came when she left school. The Clergyman who had been her father's friend asked her to become a Sunday School Teacher. Most common-place of beginnings; but to be made great or insignificant as the soul is in the man or the woman. Life palpitates round a class in a City Sunday School; and through her class Noel entered the streets of the City of Humanity.

In her group of small black girls she began to touch Life, the Sores of Reality. Every one of the half dozen existences that the school brought to her feet, led her away in a different direction It is not only when the road ascends Life's sunny slopes that the interest of variation begins. Variety lies also below, in the shadow, on the lowlands of Poverty; the apparent sameness and monotony there are an appearance only; reality lies beneath these, a different thing to its covering.

And so a year passed; and Noel at seventeen was beginning to be talked of by many in Kingston; with admiration by some, with wonder by others. She was to all appearance a lonely girl, often seen by herself; in fact seldom otherwise; and that this should be the case with one so beautiful and so manifestly gifted made most men, and specially most women, marvel.

Sometimes she went about with her Mother; very occasionally she was seen with a friend; but for the most part she was alone, whether walking or driving. She was known in the lanes where her scholars lived; and on the country roads beyond Kingston, where she was wont to travel great distances alone. Yet she was unfriendly to no one. She gave none the feeling that she wished definitely to avoid man or woman; and perhaps the explanation of her proneness to be alone was that she never felt alone.

To her it was the most natural thing possible to sit by herself in the Study, or on the Verandah; to take her way through the City; or to roam along a quiet road, fully occupied with her thoughts and observations; with these about her as friends, and with a sense of fellowship and remembrance, she did not live a life dependent on words, and so showed in contrast with our modern life which is a great waste of Speech with oases of Silence.

"Alone, Miss Bronvola?" a young man would say to her sometimes, in surprize.

"But I do not feel alone," she would reply, telling the simple truth.

Still, inevitably, she had to make friends; and one day she said;

"Mother, I am making a friend."

"Making? so the process is not complete?" said her mother, smiling.

"No, Mother, it is not. But you know who it is," and she told her mother his name.

"Your father was his father's friend," said her mother; and that for the present was the end of the matter.

But on an evening, a month later, while they both sat on the Verandah, to which Noel had just returned from playing dreamy, haunting music on the hall piano, a visitor came. It was the Young Man.

"This is my friend, Mother," said Noel, who had gone forward to receive him in the Drawing Room: and thus the door was opened to many such evenings; and so that night the vacant chair was filled; but when her Friend left, though her Mother bade her good night and went to bed, Noel returned and sat for a long time beside her Father's chair on the Verandah, with a spirit within her that was deeply, though vaguely, moved. But it was of her Father she thought; not of the Young Man, of whom she was making a friend. Thought of her Father was generally an atmosphere of her soul, rather than a distinct effort. But on this night her spirit was strangely stirred.

For long she sat in silence and perfectly still; then rising and leaning over the Verandah's Vine-crowded rail she watched the street till it grew utterly empty, as the City sank towards midnight's deeper silence and rest.

She came back and sat again beside her Father's empty chair, leaning her head on its arm. Closing her eyes, she tried to fancy she felt his hand resting on her hair and caressing it. Seldom did she feel him not so sufficiently with her, but that it was needless to invoke him by the effort definite and direct: but tonight the yearning for more than spiritual communion; the longing to feel his hand of flesh and blood as once she had felt it; to see his brown eyes, fixed up on her, lighting slowly into smiles; to rise and kiss him; to hear him speak—the longing, moved her soul through and through; and it grew to an agony that was unendurable.

She loosened her hair; and it fell in long length, a dark flood about her white, tense face. The Moon, unclouded, rising above the trees poured its beams over those fine waves of hair that framed the face so full of strong, healthy life and beauty. She looked up with eyes bright with unshed tears. The eyes he had loved; the hair he had fondled; the eyes into which he had so often smiled; the lips which he had kissed; all the life of this beautiful creature that he had given, seemed beckoning him to return to her; to return to her from the land of the Spiritual and Unseen,—once again to put on Mortality; once again to inhabit flesh and blood. The call of a Soul yet in the body for a return of the Soul that has lain down the flesh and passed to the immortal. The call so terrible because so futile. The hour when the unreason of the flesh triumphs, and to its triumph itself brings defeat. Rushing to the very brink of the depth it hears only the echo of its cry returned from the abyss of Night. While Horror and Despair creep out upon it, ready to strike it from that dizzy edge. For there indeed Despair and Horror face the Soul in their most hideous shapes; like survivals of primeval monsters, no longer encountered where men live and move; but which, frightful in appearance and deadly in power, still make their lair among the flame-scarred crags and cliffs of desolate heights, regions all but never trodden by the foot of man. There on the sudden they meet the infrequent Intruder; and in the moment of that terrible meeting strike him dead.

Noel rose at length, and taking a Lamp went into the Study, and there her Father seemed to welcome her She took down book after book that he had used, reading the lines underscored here and there. Every now and then a sentence flashed like a sun-smiten jewel; and through the influence of these thoughts he seemed to come; gently leading her back from that mood so dangerous, so horrifying, when the flesh demands with fury what the flesh can never more have; leading her back to the paths that the spirit finds and treads from life to life through death. Her wildness sank; the agony of longing receded; and he who in that agony had seemed dying away from her into a far distance, now, in the calm and ebb of her passion, returned: in part, she was comforted.

Flung abroad from the old Church Tower, the single stroke proclaiming that the first hour of a new day was completed, rolled loudly and heavily over the sleeping City. It found Noel once again Mistress of her Soul.

III

Becka

*"When Thou rememberest of what toys
We make our joys."*

Over that part of the fence which was mended with kerosene tins, cut open and nailed flat to hide the holes in the boards, Mrs. Gyrton looked into her sister Rosabella's yard, and spoke her mind; of which a bit ran thus:

"Which it is not, Rosabella, becausen you have pickney dat is good as buckra to look at, an' its Poopa is a buckra out-an'-out—not becausen of dat,—you fe lick down me chicken."

Rosabella sat at her door nursing her baby; and she answered with the feeling of a General who knows he has the strongest position, and that the Other Man must excite himself a great deal, and fail in the end. She said:

"You can't done fe talk, noh—you nigger woman is——"

"Nigger woman," interrupted Mrs. Gyrton with such indignation as made her almost grind her teeth, for she was a passionate woman. "Nigger! Oh, Lord, me God, what is dis? Me dead Mooma, me Poopa, dat Buckra put in a lockup, an' to dis day I don't know weh him deh, if him dead else him live—don't Rosabella an' I born one way? If I nigger, you nigger. What more nigger I can nigger dan you?"

Rosabella went on looking at her baby as it tugged at her breast.

"You can't ebber tink say, causen you got baby fe Buckra you whiter dan me, you own born sister; one Teeta, one Mooma. You kyant fool so. You kyant fool so, Rosabella."

"Well," said Rosabella returning to the chicken, "why you can't keep you chicken out a me yard?"

"Fe who yard?" demanded Mrs. Gyrton. Former battles had taught her to note with very great nicety the words Rosabella employed.

"Fe who yard? Weh you get yard; eider money fe buy yard?"

"For I an' Mista Stanley, of course" replied Rosa with dignity.

"Well, I tank God, an Big Missis who did teach me to be servant at Big House, dat I don't get pickney nearly white. I is a married woman."

"Married to a Carpenter," sneered Rosabella.

"I married doh, an' you lib in sin; an' hell da hot fe you."

"You is dah talk after what Buckra tell you" said Rosa disdainfully. "Weh you husban' is?"

"You know him gone look work in a Colon," said Mrs. Gyrton, a sudden touch of deprecation softening her voice; but her sister was implacable.

"I know he is a drunkard man; an' dat him lazy wuss dan man ebber lazy since man stan up an' shake himself. I know him is a tief—"

"Tek you d——mout off him," broke in the wife, "Causen I speak an tell you not fe kill me chicken you raise pon dis piece of an abusen."

"I know seh," pursued the relentless one, "I hear de two a' you jam and blarse', and blarse' and jam, till dog outside stan a you gate mout an' howl, an' rooster start cackle and crow."

"You got's no right fe lick down me chicken," persisted the Carpenter's mate doggedly. As regarded the Carpenter she knew the case was hopeless; but she stood on her undoubted rights as regarded the Chicken, and behind an entrenchment of undisputed fact.

Rosabella was quiet a minute, then she said;

"Well, an' I woulden lick it, if it would satisfy fe walk bout de yard an' pick up what him fine'. But when it come to jump pon me drawing room table, I mus' lick him; an' I wish to King it was him neck I bruck, an' not him leg lonely, when I fire de piece of wood at him."

"An' suppose I did lick down you *maugre* dog when it come slap in a me kitchen, and tief out me bit and fippance tripe I just buy."

"Dat you nebber see," returned Rosa, gathering her things together for a retreat; she noted something which as yet was unseen by her sister. That person all unconscious of developments in her rear burst out:

"See him too jam well"—but as Rosabella vanished, Mrs. Gyrton turned, for the gate of her yard had opened, and a white girl came across.

The face was a delightful one to contemplate at any time, as was the graceful young figure, lithe and erect: but the Girl seemed particularly attractive amid the sordid surroundings of that poor yard and beside the temper-furrowed and the harsh time roughened countenance of Mrs. Gyrton. The white girl with her finely moulded features, in her dress of simple white relieved by pink, appeared in the midst of the unlovely common-place of that Kingston Slum like an Angel of the Ideal. It was Noel.

"I have come only for a minute, Mrs. Gyrton" she began brightly, "to wish you a Merry Christmas. It is the day after tomorrow, you know; and I won't see you before the day comes. I have brought this for Rebecca. Can I see her?"

Rebecca was out, and Mrs. Gyrton said so.

"Well," replied Noel, "that may be all the better. It is a doll, and I wish it to be quite a surprise. You must keep it wrapped up as it is, and give it to her on Christmas morning itself. Here it is; I will open it and show it to you at once. Then you must keep it wrapped and tied for Becka, till Christmas Day."

Mrs. Gyrton promised solemnly; and after a minute or two Noel departed. She was Rebecca's Sunday School Teacher, and her very good friend.

Mrs. Gyrton, after seeing her ceremoniously to the gate, and carefully closing that rather shaky framework, came across to the weak place in the fence, and called:

"Bella, Bella."

Her sister appeared; and the Carpenter's wife enquired anxiously:

"You tink seh she hear me when I did jam you jus' now?"

"I can't tell," said Rosabella languidly; and then with woman's readiness to be unpleasant to woman, she added; "but she did bound to hear you; de way you halla it."

"I wish to Master she don't," said Mrs. Gyrton. "It all come troo you, Bella" she added.

But now Rosabella was weary of battle, and only asked:

"What dat she give you?"

"It is fe Becka."

"A what?"

"China Baby, me lub."

"Oh, Dolly" said Bella; for dolly it is in Whiteman's phraseology and "China Baby" in the saying of the Black; Bella affected, as a matter of course the Whiteman's style.

"How it stan?" she enquired.

Mrs. Gyrten on this promptly untied the string and displayed the doll, saying as she did so:

"She beg me quite hard not to open it, neider gib it to Becka till Christmas Day; an' I pramise her particular on de matter."

The two examined the Doll carefully and with curiosity. Blended with Rosabella's curiosity, was the more directly practical desire to decide whether such a doll would be good enough for her atom of coloured humanity when it was old enough to have dolls.

But in Mrs. Gyrton the mood was more reflective and philosophic. She said:—

"Bella, what you tink? Backra dont hab time to trow way; wen dem sit down good, good, and mek ting like 'a dis? It is white man and white woman got little or nutting to do."

Bella, busy with excursions into the Future, merely grunted; and indeed nothing beyond a grunt was needed in response to a remark embodying a truth so patent to the Negro at least; namely, that it is the lot of the Whiteman to play and enjoy himself, and of the Blackman to work and do only that which is useful. For in the West Indies, where the refrain of every White author is "the negro wont work," it is amusing to note that the opinion of the said Negro is set in just the opposite direction. "Blackmen," he says, "are born to work; but Backras to please themselves;" and again, he says: "It is only Backra got time to sit down an do nutting—and who get money all de same."

Mrs. Gyrton's reflections next took a moral and religious turn.

"You know, seh, Rosabella, I dont tink Backra should make likeness of live Pickney so. Why, me King, dis China Baby you might tink it was da got alk. Him got han, him got eye; him can move dem; him got shoes; him to got stocking. Big Massa gib dem true true, pickney, what de debil deh mus' go mek up play play one for. I bet you if it was Nigger shorance so Big Massa would a' open him han so box fe we head off. But Backra a' Young Massa; and Nigger a' servant boy. All de same, I tell you, dem can tek it too far; an one a dis day Backra *will* tek it too far: and you will see a piece of a trouble. Me Master, but what dem Whiteman lef' to do now? save and except build road and drive buggy go slap a heaven."

"It is a good dolly," said Rosabella, who had now reached the end of her thoughts on the matter of the Doll's value, and desired in thus expressing her opinion to convey the patent fact that she, and not her sister, was competent to pronounce on such a thing as "a dolly."

The Carpenter's Wife, still full of forebodings of the trouble in store for the "shorance Backra" who "went too far with Big Massa," failed to perceive the intention of Rosabella's remark; but, with the sadness of the Author who feels his best thoughts are not getting fairplay, she muttered the rest of her comments, doing her duty to the world by expressing them, but dismally certain that Rosabella was paying no attention whatever.

"But de hard ting is dis," she continued, "when Big Massa get mad an' bex wid dem shorance Backra, and him tek him Volcano, else him

Hurricane, else him Comic (Comet) an' mek to bruck dem up and sweep dem out, him nebber stop to tink say Blackman deh all bout me foot an' dat Blackman is not man fe do nonebody any harm; but de which and de way Big Massa bex him lick down eb'ry bit, black oh, white oh, brown oh; an' dat's how poor black people in Jamaica can't get on."

Taking the doll she wrapped it in its paper covering. Entering her dirty, shabby, little house she laid the parcel on the table beside a china ornament, now chipped and broken, which long ago the Carpenter had bought to help furnish the house; for they were an ambitious couple in the days when they first launched on the somewhat treacherous seas of matrimony.

The parcel lay there waiting Becka's coming; beside it was the little girl's Bible, and a cup containing a few grains of the corn to which the Chicken, whose leg Bella had that day broken, was treated on state occasions.

Mrs. Gyrton gat her outside and continued to starch clothes.

Meantime where was Becka? and who was she?

A small black creature of nine Augusts, she was Mrs. Gyrton's only child; the only child she had ever borne; a fact that was often emphasized by Bella and other enemies of the Carpenter's wife, when, in wordy battles, the contention was, on Mrs. Gyrton's part, that she, as a married woman, was set on high above her fellows; and, on their side, that she was after all only an imitator of white people's ways; and a failure at that.

"You is a one-pickney-an-no more woman," was Rosabella's bitter taunt towards her sister; to be followed by the triumphant argument, that it was always and ever thus that Big Massa taught Black women the folly of "marrying like Backra."

Each returning Sunday saw Becka blossom out into neatness and the glory of a clean dress; but she was a ragged little figure from Monday to Saturday. Her dress roughly made of a coarse blue cloth, was allowed to become very dirty. Buttons deserted their posts, and here and there the blue cloth itself was rent and torn, showing beneath the outer dress an under garment made of calico, that had once been white.

All through the day of this story Becka had been carrying water by the bucket-ful for her mother. Their yard had a pipe; but the pipe just then gave no water. The Water Commissioners desired a payment of Rates in arrears. Mrs. Gyrton could pay no arrears; and thereupon her pipe was locked off from the main.

Under such circumstances, the Law threatens that man with dire penalties who, having still his pipe with water therein, and seeing his brother in need, gives to the thirsty soul to drink. But it is perhaps as well that, threats notwithstanding, there are persons who will transgress the sacred law of the Kingston Water Commissioners; and from some of these, rich people unmindful of their duty to other rich people, Becka's mother got water, transporting it by means of her little daughter, who, carrying the full bucket on her head, had tramped the morning hours away.

Then it was her duty to assist her mother hang out the wash clothes; to do which she had to lug from place to place a chair, wooden, very old and without a back; for with her dirty bare feet planted on the very bosom of Mother Earth, she was altogether too short to reach the clothes line; so she climbed up and stood on the chair as she arranged the wet shirts and the trousers and the jackets in the places where they should be, fastening each piece with a wooden clip, to hold it against the breeze's persistent and mischievous attempts to fling it down on the dirty yard.

Hours of this brought the afternoon; and then once more, obedient to directions from her mother, Becka resumed her bucket and set out to carry more water.

She was away on this errand when her Sunday School Teacher came to the yard; and little did she think, as she loitered just then, resting on the rough board beneh beside the water-pipe, that by so doing she was missing the sight of her much beloved Miss Noel.

Gushing from the clean brass of the pipe, and splashing into the overflowing bucket and brimming, with bubble all afloat, over the grey tin side, pleasant was the sight and the sound of the tumbling water; pleasantly ran the soft murmur of the passing breeze in the leafy trees of the Garden near by, where, round and clean and sweet-looking showed the boles of the handsome Palms; and pleasantly, as the sunbeams found them out, shone, in rich, brave, glow, the Crotons ranged along the green grass lawn.

The tired little mortal sat and watched and listened and rested many minutes; meanwhile, at Becka's home Miss Noel came and went.

IV

"Becka's Buckra Baby"

The swift mysterious instincts

* * * *

The fated and fatal moments

B ecka," said her Mother, when Becka had returned to the yard, "Miss Noel did come fe see you; and she bring you a China Baby. It is you Christmas, and she beg me quite hard not fe show you it till Monday; neider to tell you bout it; but Saturday done already; tomorrow Sunday come; next day Christmas. It come already, so I going ghee you it now, now; but you mind me, if she ax you a' Sunday School tomorrow you must talk circumspect, and dont tell no lie pon me; but mek her to understand I not going ghee you it till Monday 'cording as I promise and she tell me; for I promise her very particular."

"Yes, Mam," said Becka almost choking with the sudden joy of the thing.

"Look in a de hall, on de table. It wrap up in piece a brown paper and it tie wid green string. When you eat you dinner done, tek it."

"Yes, Mam," said Becka.

She emptied her bucket, took the little tin plate with her dinner and obediently eat the boiled banana, rice and salt fish, that she found thereon.

"Wash you plate, mind," said her Mother, catching her eye as the last morsel of food disappeared; and Becka, washing the plate, placed it to drain.

"Tek you China Baby den," said the Mother with a touch of the ceremonious. Becka took it.

Then for a whole hour she was blissfully and completely happy.

Touched by some softer feeling, her mother left her entirely alone. Rosabella came to the fence, by and by, and the Carpenter's Wife cracked a joke with her.

"Rosabella, we got backra baby, too, now, Becka got white baby same as you."

"Praps she we' have one fe true, time to come," said Aunt Rosabella graciously.

"Who can tell," assented the mother of Rebecca; "but I trus' she will marry same as Backra do, an' same as me."

Rosabella only laughed.

It was getting dark when Becka's Mother called her.

"You mus' go down Town, Becka. Mrs. Paterson tell me bout a shop out a' Sollas weh dem got some salt pork cheaper dan anyways in Kingston. It is nighst de corner a' you left han a de market. One Chinaman keep it; so you can't loss it. Something do de pork, and him da sell it fe little and nutting. It eat all right dem tell me; and so I going sen you buy a half pound; and being as you is dere you can walk go in a market and buy me some scallion and a breadfruit; and see you get it nuff."

"Yes, Mam;" and Becka forthwith got her basket.

"And, look, yah," said Mrs. Gyrton then, "dont tek you baby, bimeby it go bruk, an' Miss Noel fine' out seh I gib it you before Monday."

Becka would gladly have appealed against this decision, had she dared; but she dared not.

"An' when you come back, if I dont yah, put what you buy weh dog cant eat it in de kitchen and go a' you bed. I got to go a' Mrs. Smart to go see if she we' pay me fe de washing, and it deh chock up by Half-way Tree; so I may be well and late."

"Yes, Ma'm," said Becka monotonously, but with delight piercing suddenly, like a ray of light, into her sombre little heart. She saw that after all it was quite possible to take the doll.

Forth Becka went on her journey, empty basket in hand, the pink of propriety before her Mother's eyes. But she went up the road not down.

Hurrying along, she chose a spot where the interval between the gas lamps was longer than usual, and where it was in consequence darker than elsewhere. Quickly then she hid herself behind a clump of bush, and waited.

People went and came, unconscious of the small eyes that scanned their passing with attentiveness.

At length Mrs. Gyrton, wash clothes in hand, went by, bound for Half-way Tree. She had passed quite out of sight ere Becka crept forth. Back to the yard, she went, opened the door at the back, and a minute later had her precious "backra baby" in her loving embrace.

With the Christmas holiday so near at hand, the streets, always crowded on Saturday nights, were more than usually packed; and

Sollas Square was the centre of the densest grouping and onflowing of buyers and sellers. But, amid the noise, the dirt and the bustle, Becka was quite at home.

She made her way to the Chinaman's shop. In that, attracted by the fame of the cheap pork a crowd had gathered, and a good natured struggle proceeded among those anxious for a place before the Counter. For a time Becka declined the combat, and while awaiting a chance to edge in, played with her Doll.

"You tief," said a voice behind her, sudden, loud and rough. She turned and finding a big lout of a Boy idling by the barrels near the door, she "sucked her teeth" at him.

"Come, I going tek it away," proceeded the lout, menacingly. "You little brute, you tief it from some one who employ you."

"You is a liard," responded Becka, indignant, and ready for battle. She "cut her eyes" to show contempt and fearlessness.

"Tief! Oh," mocked the Lout. "Who tief China Baby?"

"You tell a false," cried Becka angrily. "Miss Noel gib me it for me Christmas."

"An' Christmas dont come yet," pursued her tormentor; "and what Mies Noel would gib ting like you China Baby."

"You fast long mout naygar," answered Becka with spirit, hastening, after the manner of her sex, to defend by attacking. "What business you got with my baby?"

A Market Woman turned at this juncture, attracted by the contention. She was resting her headload near by, while she tied up "change" in a handkerchief.

"Don't noyance de chile," she remonstrated. "You boy got nutting to do but use you mout. Buy what you want, me gal, and go you ways; if you follow answer boy nonsense you got fe walk a long road; an' special dese Kingston boy," she continued, "dem don't got a piece self of manners. Got's nutting to do but mock country people, an' walk roun' and roun' da 'noyance somebody."

Becka, following her champion's advice, pushed her way to the Counter, and in due time was served with the half pound of pork that she wanted, and with a box of matches that was "brata."

By that time both the Boy and Market Woman had disappeared.

Becka's next business took her to the Market itself; and there, plunged into the multitude of buyers and sellers, and wriggling her way from stall to stall, she sought diligently till she found the Breadfruit and the Scallion that experience told her would be grateful to the judgment of her Mother.

This completed the business of the evening; and left Becka free to take such pleasure as she could take. She had not a farthing to spend; but sight and sound were free to all; and to Becka the streets were as good as a Theatre.

Staring curiously into the passing cars, and mooing very slowly along the picturesquely lighted stalls, on which glittered bright tin-ware, or glowed brown buns, brown cakes, or white bread curiously plaited, she feasted eye and ear to the full.

A Street Preacher at one corner was laying himself out to describe Hell; and Becka listened to him with great interest, till a man in the crowd spoilt everything by vexing the Preacher.

"Captain," he called, "*you* don't know what Hell is like."

"The hotness," persisted the Preacher, hoping to talk down the interrupter, "the hotness of Hell, my friends—"

"Talk foolishness," said the Critic, angry the more at being overlooked, "wha you know bout place hot. I wish I could catch you on a Steamer and mek you feed furnace one night, one single night, ole man; den you would know more bout Hell and Hot."

The Critic was a Stoker, and being a man acquainted with the Realities, his gorge rose at the feeble colouring painted by this well intentioned but incapable Artist now before him.

"Brothers," said the Stoker's, Victim, "and Sisters," he added as an after thought, his eye falling on Becka, "We will now sing a hymn." He was a man, slow and patient, but not without craft, and some desire to retaliate.

"Well, sing," grumbled the Stoker, hurrying up speech before the oncoming roar of sound drowned his voice. "Sing you hymn dem; but don't talk bout Hell and Hot, when you don't know."

"Whiter than Snow" was the melody that then rose to heaven. Truly that Stoker would have taken some washing.

Becka moved on, to be attracted presently by a long and bitter disputation which proceeded at the stand of a Peppermint Seller. The matter at issue was three farthings worth of candy; but the Seller wielded a style of description and narrative that far outran, in the graphic art, the Preacher's feeble attempts; and it was a real pleasure to hear her tell the story of how the man at whom she now pointed the finger of scorn, had attempted to get her "gill worth" of peppermint "for little or nutting."

The man, poor worm, replied only just enough to inspire further castigation; and Becka lingering, listened, hugely interested, and even oblivious for whole minutes to her Buckra Baby.

Then someone jostled her; and, turning at the minute sharply she realized that the Lout had snatched at her doll. He seized it and ran up street crying:

"You tief it; you tief it. Who tief China Baby?"

Becka dashed after him, her whole soul so racked and strained that she hardly saw the horses and the buses round her; even the Electric Cars with their big head lights, their loud wheel rush and harsh sounding bells crashed by her, unregarded! She called out passionately:

"Gib me, me backra baby. Gib me, me baby," but the basket weighed her down and the Boy easily kept ahead.

So, block after block, he teazed her; and a group of people who waited at a cross street might have seen the whole of the proceedings from first to last, though in fact they noticed neither the Boy nor the Child, till the former, tired of the sport, pitched the doll with a quick toss out into mid street, where it fell across the tram line.

Then a cry of warning, blending into one of horror, rose; for, blind to all else but the fallen doll, and to every circumstance of danger, Becka ran across to the line at the very moment that a Car on the down line rushed there with a noise of harshly loud wheels The strong, intense blaze of light flung before it marked her out, like the eye of a monster searching for its prey. For the fraction of a second, the eager child's figure stood out in appalling glory, and those watching saw that of the Motorman as he strove wildly to apply the brake.

From the side of the street a White Girl, standing there with a young man, ran forward to reach Becka. Her companion, crying sharply:

"Miss Noel, it is madness," seized her arm at the same instant.

Her Will thrust his words away, as granite beats through a puff of spray; but as he realized that speech was vain he tightened his hold on her arm, till he felt her impulse recoil, curbed by the physical check. His grasp and not his words stayed her gallant motion.

Then she turned on him with eyes that blazed a deep anger such as he had never met before. Her beautiful face quivered with strength of feeling.

In the swift instant of her pause and look the terrible death of Becka was over.

Too small to be crushed, the doll lay safe and sound on the bricks where it had been tossed, except that in falling a hand had been snapped away.

Becka was a mass of quivering, bloody flesh.

The crowd swooped down on the scene at once, and word went up:

"Dead. Quite dead. A little black child."

The White Girl with eyes averted from her friend's face, waited tensely till the death was announced. Her one swift glance a minute before, which read for her the approaching catastrophe and led to her quick leap to save the child, had not revealed the identity of the victim. Noel had not recognised Becka. If the child, thought of as a stranger, was dead, nothing more could be done by her.

She turned to the young man beside her:

"I wish you to leave me," she said in a cutting tone.

"I?" he asked, astonished. "Have I offended you?—I—I—held you. I could not help it."

"You stopped me" she said.

"The danger" he urged, "you did not see it."

"I saw the danger," she replied, quietly, but in anger.

"I was too rough," he said penitently. "I hurt your arm; but I had to hold you tight to stop you."

"You stopped me" was her reply to that.

"I prevented you killing yourself" he returned with a touch of impatience.

"The child was killed," she answered.

"You could not have saved her." He spoke like one applying cold Fact and plain Common Sense to Fancy if not Fantasy.

"There was a chance." The girl said "I would have tried."

"And have been killed."

"A life for a life," she said; and she in her turn was now impatient. "Good night."

He would have been a wise man to have left her then, at once, with not a word further: for in truth she needed solitude. But how few are the young men who are wise. He persisted and cast himself over the precipice.

"Your life against hors," he answered hotly and angrily; "a child like that; and you. My dear Miss Noel, don't be unreasonable. I apologise for touching you; but it was the only way to stop you."

"I should not have been stopped," said the Girl, so quietly that apart from the blood of the child on the street, you might have thought she jested. But she was in deadly earnest.

THOMAS MACDERM

"You mean that? You should not have been stopped?" he exclaimed. "You are quite unreasonable."

"We will not argue it," she said, with a deepened cadence of intensity.

"But it was a most serious thing."

"It matters, because it was so serious," she answered at once.

"You did not see—You did not understand."

"I saw everything. I understood, and I could have stopped myself had I wished to. No one else should have stopped me." She repeated her "Good night," and turned very slightly from him.

He flushed; looked at her, and a ugly flame of the hate born of a miscomprehension of motive flashed momentarily in his eyes. It is the Hate most uncompromizing, most deadly. Then it sank and he said, pleading:

"Don't be unjust, Miss Noel." Then after a pause "Don't be unreasonable." Then almost with humility, "I did it for the best."

She did not answer.

"At any rate" he said, "let me wait till your car comes."

"I would prefer you to leave me, now."

Then, he lifted his hat and left her, conscious in a dim way that his dream was over.

The first man attracted by this girl's soul had made his failure to enter into communion with her spirit.

And Noel! she stood alone, waiting for her car, filled with the strongest indignation; a girl so beautiful in her young womanhood, so erect and strong in her youth, that even apart from the charm of her finely moulded features, the firm but lovely lips, the complexion delicately clear, eyes, brown, bright, and of perfect vision, hair dark and wavy, her truly proportioned form, she had a charm potent to attract and influence any spirit that could respond to Beauty, Purity and Grace.

She was one of those women about whom the Spirit of Life seems a penetrating, a pervading, almost a visible influence; so that, it is really by an after thought that you note the beautiful face and the graceful form.

Noel did not know that the little mangled body had any special claim on her interest. She was ignorant for the present of the tragedy induced by her Christmas gift; but she quivered to the last fibre of her being at the thought that the sacrifice her *willing* heart, in that moment of high realization, had leapt to make, had been crudely and roughly pushed back from the very foot of the Altar.

And late that night when Becka's Mother and her Aunt Rosabella were wailing their dead; and waiting for the morning that they might send and tell Miss Noel of their trouble, Noel, in her dainty bedroom, sat wide awake in the darkness at the window. She looked out into the night, watching the stars burning in their far off homes, and looking from them to the City's feeble fires; and she could not sleep, nor could she rest.

And, behold, her thought was not that she had escaped by her friend's ready hand frightful mutilation; but that they were ever divided as friends because by his hand she had been restrained from giving her life for another.

It was her destiny to cross the years and to enter Womanhood; but had her choice that night been fulfilled her splendid life would have been spilt in red drops on the threshold; or flung, on lintelland doorpost, a crimson Passover mark to wave back the Angel of Death from a life that he had claimed.

To Youth is excess of thought and of emotion; and to Youth, from the angle of an older world, and a world that claims to be wiser, unreason, even absurdity is charged in its, actions and impulses of nobility. But who will say that this girl was unreasonable who, full of life's happiest, fullest pulse, leapt to obey an instinct that had been given to her, deepest of any in her nature.

But the episode of "Becka's Buckra Baby," which we have now watched to its conclusion, came not to end but, for good or for evil, to begin the Life of Noel, a girl unlike and yet most deeply like other girls; to an attention to whose fortunes the reader may some day be called by the present writer Meantime let us leave her, recovering strength and composure, in the hours of darkness leading out to the Dawn, during the moments when her soul swayed and shook as, with the tremor of deep currents, vibrates an ocean full to the shore-lip, brooded over by Night and Silence, and watched by Stars, large, strong and serene.

The End of the Episode

A Note About the Author

Thomas MacDermot (1870–1933) was a Jamaican poet, novelist, and newspaper editor. Born in Clarendon Parish, he was raised in a family of five children in Trelawny. After receiving his education at Falmouth Academy and at the Church of England Grammar School in Kingston, he remained in the capital to teach and become a journalist. Starting at *The Jamaica Post* and *The Daily Gleaner*, he moved to the *Jamaica Times*, where he would serve as editor for twenty years. In 1899, he launched a popular short story contest for young writers, helping further the careers of famed poet Claude McKay and journalist H. G. de Lisser. By 1903, he established *All Jamaica Library*, a low-cost series of short fiction by Jamaican authors. MacDermot also wrote his own works of fiction under the anagrammatic penname "Tom Redcam." *Becka's Buckra Baby* (1903) is considered a landmark of Jamaican literature and helped distinguish the Caribbean as a hotspot for modern writing. Following his death in England, MacDermot was posthumously appointed Jamaica's first Poet Laureate.

A Note from the Publisher

Spanning many genres, from non-fiction essays to literature classics to children's books and lyric poetry, Mint Edition books showcase the master works of our time in a modern new package. The text is freshly typeset, is clean and easy to read, and features a new note about the author in each volume. Many books also include exclusive new introductory material. Every book boasts a striking new cover, which makes it as appropriate for collecting as it is for gift giving. Mint Edition books are only printed when a reader orders them, so natural resources are not wasted. We're proud that our books are never manufactured in excess and exist only in the exact quantity they need to be read and enjoyed.

Discover more of your favorite classics with Bookfinity™.

- Track your reading with custom book lists.
- Get great book recommendations for your personalized Reader Type.
- Add reviews for your favorite books.
- AND MUCH MORE!

Visit **bookfinity.com** and take the fun Reader Type quiz to get started.

Enjoy our classic and modern companion pairings!

www.ingramcontent.com/pod-product-compliance
Lightning Source LLC
Chambersburg PA
CBHW020610130626
46552CB00007B/3143